Anthony Horowitz was brought up on horror stories, and his childhood love of all things sinister and scary has stayed with him. The stories in this book are inspired by ordinary, everyday objects and events, as are most of the stories in the rest of the series. But each of them has a twist to remind us that even in a safe, predictable world, the horrible and unexpected, the blood-curdling and the spine-chilling, are never far away.

Anthony Horowitz is the highly successful author of a bestselling range of books, including detective stories, adventure stories and spy stories which have been translated into over a dozen languages. He is also a well-known television screenwriter with credits including *Poirot, Midsomer Murders* and *Foyle's War*. Anthony lives in East London.

'A first class children's novelist'
TIMES EDUCATIONAL SUPPLEMENT

'Perfect for readers with an appetite for ghoulish happenings'
SCHOOL LIBRARIAN ASSOCIATION

'Suspenseful and exciting'
BOOKS FOR KEEPS

KILLER CAMERA

To Stefan Kinner.

A man of many parts.

Orchard Books
338 Euston Road, London NW1 3BH
Orchard Books Australia
Hachette Children's Books
Level 17/207 Kent Street, Sydney, NSW 2000

First published by Orchard Books in 1999
This edition published in 2008
Text copyright © Anthony Horowitz 1999

A CIP catalogue record for this book is available from the British Library

ISBN 978 1 84616 971 7

3 5 7 9 10 8 6 4

www.orchardbooks.co.uk

Printed and bound in Great Britain by CPI Bookmarque, Croydon, CR0 4TD

Orchard Books is a division of Hachette Children's Books,
an Hachette Livre UK company.

ANTHONY HOROWITZ

KILLER CAMERA

ORCHARD BOOKS

Contents

KILLER
camera

The car-boot sale took place every Saturday on the edge of Crouch End.

There was a patch of empty land there; not a car park, not a building site, just a square of rubble and dust that nobody seemed to know what to do with. And then one summer the car-boot sales had arrived like flies at a picnic and since then there'd been one every week. Not that there was anything very much to buy. Cracked glasses and hideous plates, mouldy paperback books by writers you'd never heard of, electric kettles and bits of hi-fi that looked forty years out of date.

Matthew King decided to go in only because it was free. He'd visited the car-boot sale before and the only thing he'd come away with was a cold. But this was a warm Saturday afternoon. He had plenty of time. And, anyway, it was there.

But it was the same old trash. He certainly wasn't going to find his father a fiftieth birthday present here, not unless the old man had a sudden yearning for a five-hundred-piece Snow White jigsaw puzzle (missing one piece) or an electric coffee maker (only slightly cracked) or perhaps a knitted cardigan in an unusual shade of pink (aaaagh!).

Matthew sighed. There were times when he hated living in London and this was one of them. It was only after his own birthday, his fourteenth, that his parents had finally agreed to let him go out on his own. And it was only then that he realised he didn't really have anywhere to go. Crummy Crouch End with its even crummier car-boot sale. Was this any place for a smart, good-looking teenager on a summer afternoon?

He was about to leave when a car pulled in and parked in the furthest corner. At first he thought it must be a mistake. Most of the cars at the sale were old and rusty, as clapped-out as the stuff they were selling. But this was a red Volkswagen, L-registration, bright red and shiny clean. As Matthew watched, a smartly dressed man stepped out, opened the boot and stood there, looking awkward and ill-at-ease, as if he were unsure what to do next. Matthew strolled over to him.

He would always remember the contents of the boot. It was strange. He had a bad memory. There was a programme on TV where you had to remember all the prizes that came out on a conveyor belt and he'd never been able to manage more than two or three but this time it stayed in his mind...well, like a photograph.

There were clothes: a baseball jacket, several pairs of jeans, T-shirts. A pair of roller blades, a Tintin rocket, a paper lampshade. Lots of books; paperbacks and a brand-new English dictionary. About twenty CDs – mainly pop, a Sony Walkman, a guitar, a box of water-colour paints, a ouija board, a Game Boy...

...and a camera.

Matthew reached out and grabbed the camera. He was already aware that a small crowd had gathered behind him and more hands were reaching past him to snatch items out of the boot. The man who had driven the car didn't move. Nor did he show any emotion. He had a round face with a small moustache and he looked fed up. He didn't want to be there in Crouch End, at the car-boot sale. Everything about him said it.

'I'll give you a tenner for this,' someone said.

Matthew saw that they were holding the baseball jacket. It was almost new and must have been worth at least thirty pounds.

'Done,' the man said. His face didn't change.

Matthew turned the camera over in his hands. Unlike the jacket, it was old, probably bought second hand, but it seemed to be in good condition. It was a Pentax – but the 'x' on the casing had worn away. That was the only sign of damage. He held it up and looked through the viewfinder. About five metres away, a woman was holding up the horrible pink cardigan he had noticed earlier. He focused and felt a certain thrill as the powerful lens seemed to carry him forward so that the cardigan now filled his vision. He could even make out the buttons – silvery white and loose. He swivelled round, the cars and the crowd racing across the viewfinder as he searched for a subject. For no reason at all he focused on a large bedroom mirror propped up against another car. His finger found the shutter release and he pressed it. There was a satisfying click, it seemed that the camera worked.

And it would make a perfect present. Only a few months before, his dad had been complaining about the pictures he'd just had back from their last holiday in France. Half of them had been out of focus and the rest of them had been so overexposed that they'd made the Loire Valley look about as enticing as the Gobi Desert on a bad day.

'It's the camera,' he'd insisted. 'It's clapped out and useless. I'm going to get myself a new one.'

But he hadn't. In one week's time he was going to be fifty years old. And Matthew had the perfect birthday present right in his hands.

How much would it cost? The camera felt expensive. For a start it was heavy. Solid. The lens was obviously a powerful one. The camera didn't have an automatic rewind, a digital display or any of the other things that came as standard these days. But technology was cheap. Quality was expensive. And this was undoubtedly a quality camera.

'Will you take ten pounds for this?' Matthew asked. If the owner had been happy to take so little for the baseball jacket, perhaps he wouldn't think twice about the camera. But this time the man shook his head. 'It's worth a hundred at least,' he said. He turned away to take twenty pounds for the guitar. It had been bought by a young black woman who strummed it as she walked away.

'I'll have a look at that...' A thin, dark-haired woman reached out to take the camera but Matthew pulled it back. He had three twenty-pound notes in his back pocket. Twelve weeks' worth of shoe-cleaning, car-washing and generally helping around the house. He hadn't meant to spend all of it on his dad. Perhaps not even half of it.

'Will you take forty pounds?' he asked the man. 'It's all I've got,' he lied.

The man glanced at him, then nodded. 'Yes. That'll do.'

Matthew felt a surge of excitement and at the same time a sudden fear. A hundred-pound camera for forty quid? It had to be broken. Or stolen. Or both. But then the woman opened her mouth to speak and Matthew quickly found his money and thrust it out. The man took it without looking pleased or sorry. He simply folded the notes and put them in his pocket as if the payment meant nothing to him.

'Thank you,' Matthew said.

The man looked straight at him. 'I just want to get rid of it,' he said. 'I want to get rid of it all.'

'Who did it belong to?'

The man shrugged. 'Students,' he said – as if the one word explained it all. Matthew waited. The crowd had separated, moving on to the other stalls, and for a moment the two of them were alone. 'I used to rent a couple of rooms,' the man explained. 'Art students. Three of them. A couple of months ago they disappeared. Just did a bunk – owing two months' rent. Bloody cheek! I've tried to find them but they haven't had the decency to call. So my wife told me to sell some of their stuff. I didn't want to. But *they're* the ones who owe *me*. It's only fair...'

A plump woman pushed between them, snatching

up a handful of the T-shirts. 'How much for these?' The sun was still shining but suddenly Matthew felt cold.

...they disappeared...

Why should three art students suddenly vanish leaving all their gear, including a hundred-pound camera, behind? The landlord obviously felt guilty about selling it. Was Matthew doing the right thing, buying it? Quickly he turned round and hurried away, before either of them changed their mind.

He had just stepped through the gates and reached the street when he heard it: the unmistakable sound of shattering glass. He turned round and looked back and saw that the bedroom mirror he had just photographed with the new camera had been knocked over. At least, he assumed that was what had happened. It was lying face-down, surrounded by splinters of glass.

The owner – a short, stocky man with a skinhead cut – bounded forward and grabbed hold of a man who had just been passing. 'You knocked over my mirror!' he shouted.

'I never went near it.' The man was younger,

wearing jeans and a Star Wars T-shirt.

'I saw you! That'll be five quid…'

'Get lost!'

And then, even as Matthew watched, the skinhead drew back his fist and lashed out. Matthew almost heard the knuckles connect with the other man's face. The second man screamed. Blood gushed out of his nose and dripped down on to his T-shirt.

Matthew drew the camera close to his chest, turned and hurried away.

'It must be stolen,' Elizabeth King said, taking the camera.

'I don't think so,' Matthew said. 'I told you what he said!'

'What did you pay for it?' Jamie asked. Jamie was his younger brother. Three years younger and wildly jealous of everything he did.

'None of your business,' Matthew replied.

Elizabeth pushed a lever on the camera with her

fingernail and the back sprang open. 'Oh look!' she said. 'There's a film in here.' She tilted the camera back and a Kodak cartridge fell into the palm of her hand. 'It's used,' she added.

'He must have left it there,' Jamie said.

'Maybe you should get it developed,' Elizabeth suggested. 'You never know what you'll find.'

'Boring family snaps,' Matthew muttered.

'It could be porn!' Jamie shouted.

'Grow up, moron!' Matthew sighed.

'You're such a nerd…!'

'Retard…'

'Come on, boys. Let's not quarrel!' Elizabeth handed the camera back to Matthew. 'It's a nice present,' she said. 'Chris will love it. And he doesn't need to know where you got it…or how you think it got there.'

Christopher King was an actor. He wasn't famous, although people still recognised him from a coffee advert he'd done two years before, but he was always in work. In this, the week before his fiftieth birthday, he was appearing as Banquo in Shakespeare's *Macbeth* ('the Scottish play', he called it – he said it was bad luck to mention the piece by name). He'd been murdered six nights – and one afternoon – a week for the past five weeks and he was beginning to look forward to the end of the run.

Both Matthew and Jamie liked it when their father was in a London play, especially if it coincided with the summer holidays. It meant they could spend quite a bit of the day together. They had an old Labrador, Polonius, and the four of them would often go out walking on Hampstead Heath. Elizabeth King worked part-time in a dress shop but if she was around she'd come too. They were a close, happy family. The Kings had been married for twenty years.

Secretly, Matthew was a little shocked about how much money he had spent on the camera but by the time the birthday arrived he had managed to put it behind him and he was genuinely pleased by his father's reaction.

'It's great!' Christopher exclaimed, turning the camera in his hands. The family had just finished breakfast and were still sitting round the table in the kitchen. 'It's exactly what I wanted. Automatic exposure *and* a light meter! Different apertures...' He looked up at Matthew who was beaming with pleasure. 'Where did you get it from, Matt? Did you rob a bank?'

'It was second hand,' Jamie announced.

'I can see that. But it's still a great camera. Where's a film?'

'I didn't get one, Dad...' Matthew remembered the film he'd found in the camera. It was on the table by his bed. Now he cursed himself. Why hadn't he thought to buy a new one? What good was a camera without a film?

'You haven't opened my present, Dad,' Jamie said.

Christopher put down the camera and reached for a small, square box, wrapped in Power Rangers paper. He tore it open and laughed as a carton of film tumbled on to the table. 'Now that was a great idea,' he exclaimed.

'Cheapskate,' Matthew thought, but wisely said nothing.

'Now, how does it go in...?'

'Here. Let me.' Matthew took the camera from his father and opened the back. Then he tore open the carton and started to lower the film into place.

But he couldn't do it.

He stopped.

And slid into the nightmare.

It was as if his family – Christopher and Elizabeth sitting at the breakfast table, Jamie hovering at their side – had become a photograph themselves. Matthew was suddenly watching them from outside, frozen in another world. Everything seemed to have stopped. At the same time he felt something that he had never felt in his life – a strange tingling at the back of his neck as, one after another, the hairs stood on end. He looked down at the camera which had become a gaping black hole in his hands. He felt himself falling, being sucked into it. And once he was inside, the back of the camera would be a coffin lid which would snap shut, locking him in the terrible darkness...

'Matt? Are you all right?' Christopher reached out and took the camera, breaking the spell, and

Matthew realised that his whole body was trembling. There was sweat on his shoulders and in the palms of his hands. What had happened to him? What had he just experienced?

'Yes. I'm...' He blinked and shook his head.

'Are you getting a summer cold?' his mother asked. 'You've gone quite pale.'

'I...'

There was a loud snap. Christopher held up the camera. 'There! It's in!'

Jamie climbed on to his chair and stuck one leg out like a statue, showing off. 'Take me!' he called out. 'Take a picture of me!'

'I can't. I haven't got a flash.'

'We can go out in the garden!'

'There's not enough sun.'

'Well you've got to take something, Chris,' Elizabeth said.

In the end Christopher took two pictures. It didn't matter what the subjects were, he said. He just wanted to experiment.

First of all he took a picture of a tree, growing in the

middle of the lawn. It was the cherry tree that Elizabeth had planted while he was appearing in Chekhov's *The Cherry Orchard* just after they were married. It had flowered every year since.

And then, when Jamie had persuaded Polonius, the Labrador, to waddle out of his basket and into the garden, Christopher took a picture of him as well.

Matthew watched all this with a smile but refused to take part. He was still feeling sick. It was as if he had been half-strangled or punched in the pit of his stomach. He reached out and poured himself a glass of apple juice. His mother was probably right. He must be going down with flu.

But he forgot about it later when two more actors from 'the Scottish play' called round and they all went out for an early lunch. After that, Christopher caught a bus into town – it was a Wednesday and he had to be at the theatre by two – and Matthew spent the rest of the afternoon playing computer games with Polonius asleep at the foot of his bed.

It was two days later that his mother noticed it.

'Look at that!' she exclaimed, gazing out of the kitchen window.

'What's that?' Christopher had been sent a new play and he was reading it before his audition.

'The cherry tree!'

Matthew walked over to the window and looked out. He saw at once what his mother meant. The tree was about three metres tall. Although the best of the blossom was over, it had already taken on its autumn colours, a great burst of dark red leaves fighting for attention on the delicate branches. At least, that was how it had been the day before.

Now the cherry tree was dead. The branches were bare, the leaves, brown and shrivelled, scattered over the lawn. Even the trunk seemed to have turned grey and the whole tree was bent over like a sick, old man.

'What's happened?' Christopher opened the kitchen door and walked out into the garden. Elizabeth followed him. He reached the tree and scooped up a handful of the leaves. 'It's completely dead!' he exclaimed.

'But a tree can't just...die.' Matthew had never

seen his mother look so sad and he suddenly realised that the cherry must have been more than a tree to her. It had grown alongside her marriage and her family. 'It looks as if it's been poisoned!' she muttered.

Christopher dropped the leaves and wiped his hand on his sleeve. 'Perhaps it was something in the soil,' he said. He pulled Elizabeth towards him. 'Cheer up! We'll plant another one.'

'But it was special. *The Cherry Orchard...*'

Christopher put an arm round his wife. 'At least I took a picture of it,' he said. 'It means we've got something to remember it by.'

The two of them went back into the house leaving Matthew alone in the garden. He reached out and ran a finger down the bark of the tree. It felt cold and slimy to the touch. He shivered. He had never seen anything that looked quite so...dead.

'*At least I took a picture of it...*'

Christopher's words echoed in his mind. He suddenly felt uneasy – but he didn't know why.

The accident happened the next day.

Matthew wasn't up yet. Lying in bed, he heard first

27

the sound of the front door crashing open – too hard – and then the voices echoing up the stairs towards him.

'Liz! What is it? What's the matter?'

'Oh Chris!' Matthew froze. His mother never cried. Never. But she was crying now. 'It's Polonius...'

'What happened?'

'I don't know! I don't understand it!'

'Lizzie, he's not...'

'He is. I'm sorry. I'm so sorry...' That was all she could say.

In the kitchen, Christopher made tea and listened to the cold facts. Elizabeth had walked down into Crouch End to get the newspaper and post some letters. She had taken Polonius with her. As usual, the Labrador had padded after her. She never put him on a lead. He was well-trained. He never ran into the road, even if he saw a cat or a squirrel. The truth was that, aged nearly twelve, Polonius hardly ever ran at all.

But today, for no reason, he had suddenly walked off the pavement. Elizabeth hadn't even seen him until it was too late. She had opened her mouth to call his name when the Landrover had appeared, driving too fast round the corner. All the cars drove too fast on Wolseley Road. Elizabeth had closed her eyes at the last moment. But she had heard the yelp, the terrible thump, and she had known that Polonius could not have survived.

At least it had been quick. The driver of the Landrover had been helpful and apologetic. He had taken the dog to the vet...to be buried or cremated or whatever. Polonius was gone. He had been with the family since he was a puppy and now he was gone.

Lying in bed, Matthew listened to his parents talking and although he didn't hear all of it he knew enough. He rested his head on the pillow, his eyes brimming with tears. 'You took a picture of him,' he muttered to himself. 'A picture is all we have left.'

And that was when he knew.

At the car-boot sale, Matthew had taken a picture of a mirror. The mirror had smashed.

His father had taken a picture of the cherry tree.

29

The cherry tree had died.

Then he'd taken a picture of Polonius...

Matthew turned to one side, his cheek coming into contact with the cool surface of the pillow. And there it was, where he had left it, on the table by his bed. The film that he had found inside the camera when he bought it. The film that had already been exposed.

That afternoon, he took it to the chemist and had it developed.

There were twenty-four pictures in the packet.

Matthew had bought himself a Coke in a café in Crouch End and now he tore the packet open, letting the glossy pictures slide out on to the table. For a moment he hesitated. It felt wrong, stealing this glimpse into somebody else's life...like a Peeping Tom. But he had to know.

The first ten pictures only made him feel worse. They showed a young guy, in his early twenties, and somehow Matthew knew that this was the owner of the camera. He was kissing a pretty, blonde girl in one picture, throwing a cricket ball in another.

`*Art students. Three of them...*'

The man at the car-boot sale had rented part of his house to art students. And this must be them. Three of them. The camera owner. The blonde girl. And another guy, thin, with long hair and uneven teeth.

Matthew shuffled quickly through the rest of the pictures.

An exhibition of paintings. A London street. A railway station. A beach. A fishing boat. A house...

The house was different. It was like nothing Matthew had ever seen before. It stood, four storeys high, in the ruins of a garden, slanting out of a tangle of nettles and briars with great knife-blades of grass stabbing at the brickwork. It was obviously deserted, empty. Some of the windows had been smashed. The black paint was peeling in places, exposing brickwork that glistened like a suppurating wound.

Closer. A cracked gargoyle leered at the camera, arching out over the front door. The door was a massive slab of oak, its iron knocker shaped like a pair of baby's arms with the hands clasped.

Six people had come to the house that night. There was a picture of them, grouped together in the garden. Matthew recognised the three students from art school. Now they were all dressed in black shirts, black jeans. Two more men and another girl, all aged about twenty, stood behind them. One of the men had raised his arms and was grimacing, doing a vampire impersonation. They were all laughing. Matthew wondered if a seventh person had taken the picture or if it had been set to automatic. He turned over the next photograph and was taken into the house.

Click. A vast entrance hall. Huge flagstones and, in the distance, the rotting bulk of a wooden staircase twisting up to nowhere.

Click. The blonde girl drinking red wine. Drinking it straight from the bottle.

Click. A guy with fair hair holding two candles. Behind him another guy holding a paintbrush.

Click. The flagstones again, but now they've painted a white circle on them and the guy with fair hair is adding words. But you can't read the words.

They've been wiped out by the reflection from the flash.

Click. More candles. Flickering now. Placed round the circle. Three members of the group holding hands.

Click. They're naked! They've taken off their clothes. Matthew can see everything but at the same time he sees nothing. He doesn't believe it. It's madness...

Click. A cat. A black cat. Its eyes have caught the flash and have become two pinpricks of fire. The cat has sharp, white teeth. It is snarling, writhing in the hands that hold it.

Click. A knife.

Matthew closed his eyes. He knew now what they were doing. At the same time he remembered the other object that the man had been selling at the car-boot sale. He had noticed it at the time but hadn't really thought about it. The ouija board. A game for people who like to play with things they don't understand. A game for people who aren't afraid of the dark. But Matthew was afraid.

Sitting there in the cafe with the photographs spread out in front of him, he couldn't bring himself to believe it. But there could be no escaping the truth. A group of students had gone to an abandoned house. Perhaps they'd taken some sort of book with them; an old book of spells…they could have found it in an antiques shop. Matthew had once seen something like that in the shop where his mother worked: an old, leather-bound book with yellowing pages and black, splattery handwriting. A grimoire, she'd called it. The people in the photograph must have found one somewhere and, tired of the ouija board, they'd decided to do something more dangerous, more frightening. To summon up…

What?

A ghost? A demon?

Matthew had seen enough horror films to recognise what the photographs showed. A magic circle. Candles. The blood of a dead cat. The six people had taken it all very seriously – even stripping naked for the ritual. And they had succeeded. Somehow Matthew knew that the ritual had worked.

That they had raised...something. And it had killed them.

'*They disappeared. Just did a bunk...*'

The man at the car-boot sale had never seen them again. Of course, they'd returned to his house, to wherever it was they rented. If they hadn't gone back, the camera would never have been there. But after that, something must have happened. Not to one of them. But to all of them.

The camera...

Matthew looked down at the prints. He had worked his way through the pile but there were still three or four pictures left. He reached out with his fingers to separate them but then stopped. Had the student who owned the camera taken a picture of the creature, the thing, whatever it was they had summoned up with their spells? Was it there now, on the table in front of him? Could it be possible...?

He didn't want to know.

Matthew picked up the entire pile and screwed them up in his hands. He tried to tear them but couldn't. Suddenly he felt sick and angry. He hadn't wanted any of this. He had just wanted a birthday present for his father and he had brought something horrible and evil into the house. One of the photographs slipped through his fingers and...

...something red, glowing, two snake eyes, a huge shadow...

...Matthew saw it out of the corner of his eye even as he tried not to look at it. He grabbed hold of the picture and began to tear it, once, twice, into ever-smaller pieces.

'Are you all right, love?'

The waitress had appeared from nowhere and stood over the table looking down at Matthew. Matthew half smiled and opened his hand, scattering fragments of the photograph. 'Yes...' He stood up. 'I don't want these,' he said.

'I can see that. Shall I put them in the bin for you?'

'Yes. Thanks...'

The waitress swept up the crumpled photographs and the torn pieces and carried them over to the bin. When she turned round again, the table was empty. Matthew had already gone.

•

Find the camera. Smash the camera. The two thoughts ran through his mind again and again. He would explain it to his father later. Or maybe he wouldn't. How could he tell him what he now knew to be true?

'You see, Dad, this guy had the camera and he used it in some sort of black-magic ritual. He took a picture of a demon and the demon either killed him or frightened him away and now it's *inside* the camera. Every time you take a picture with the camera you kill whatever you're aiming at. Remember the cherry tree? Remember Polonius? And there was this mirror too…'

Christopher would think he was mad. It would be better not even to try to explain. He would just take the camera and lose it. Perhaps at the bottom of a canal. His parents would think someone had stolen it. It would be better if they never knew.

He arrived home. He had his own keys and let himself in.

He knew at once that his parents had gone out.

The coats were missing in the hall and, apart from the sound of hoovering coming from upstairs, the house felt empty. As he closed the front door, the hoovering stopped and a short, round woman appeared at the top of the stairs. Her name was Mrs Bayley and she came in twice a week to help Elizabeth with the cleaning.

'Is that you, Matthew?' she called down. She relaxed when she saw him. 'Your mum said to tell you she'd gone out.'

'Where did she go?' Matthew felt the first stirrings of alarm.

'Your dad took her and Jamie up to Hampstead Heath. And that new camera you bought him. He said he wanted to take their picture...'

And that was it. Matthew felt the floor tilt underneath him and he slid back, his shoulders hitting the wall.

The camera.

Hampstead Heath.

Not Mum! Not Jamie!

'What's the matter?' Mrs Bayley came down the

stairs towards him. 'You look as if you've seen a ghost!'

'I have to go there!' The words came out as a gabble. Matthew forced himself to slow down. 'Mrs Bayley. Have you got your car? Can you give me a lift?'

'I still haven't done the kitchen...'

'Please! It's important!'

There must have been something in his voice. Mrs Bayley looked at him, puzzled. Then she nodded. 'I can take you up if you like. But the Heath's a big place. I don't know how you're going to find them...'

She was right, of course. The Heath stretched all the way from Hampstead to Highgate and down to Gospel Oak, a swathe of green that rose and fell with twisting paths, ornamental lakes and thick clumps of woodland. Walking on the Heath, you hardly felt you were in London at all and even if you knew where you were going it was easy to get lost. Where would they have gone? They could be anywhere.

Mrs Bayley had driven him down from Highgate in her rusting Fiat Panda and was about to reach the first main entrance when he saw it, parked next to a bus stop. It was his father's car. There was a sticker in the back window – LIVE THEATRE MAKES LIFE BETTER – and the bright red letters jumped out at him. Matthew had always been a little embarrassed by that stupid line. Now he read the words with a flood of relief.

'Stop here, Mrs Bayley!' he shouted.

Mrs Bayley twisted the steering wheel and there was the blare of a horn from behind them as they swerved into the side of the road. 'Have you seen them?' she asked.

'Their car. They must be up at Kenwood...'

Kenwood House. It was one of the most beautiful sights of the Heath; a white, eighteenth-century building on a gentle rise, looking down over a flat lawn and a lake. It was just the sort of place where Christopher might have gone for a walk...

Gone to take a picture.

Matthew scrambled out of the car, slamming the door behind him. Already he could imagine Elizabeth and Jamie with their backs to the house. Christopher standing with the camera. 'A little closer. Now smile...' His finger would stab downwards – and then what? Matthew remembered the cherry tree, colourless and dead. Polonius, who had never stepped into the road before. The mirror, smashing at the car-boot sale. A gush of blood from the fight it had provoked. Even as he ran along the pavement and swung through the first entrance to the Heath he wondered if he wasn't mad, if he hadn't imagined the whole thing. But then he remembered the pictures: the empty house, the candles.

The shadow. Two burning red eyes…

And Matthew knew that he was right, that he had imagined none of it, and that he had perhaps only minutes in which to save his father, his mother, his younger brother.

If it wasn't too late already.

Christopher, Elizabeth and Jamie weren't at Kenwood. They weren't on the terrace, or on the lawn. Matthew ran from one end of the house to the other, pushing through the crowds, ignoring the cries of protest. He thought he saw Jamie in the ornamental gardens and pounced on him – but it was another boy, nothing like his brother. The whole world seemed to have smashed (like the mirror at the car-boot sale) as he forced himself on, searching for his family. He was aware only of the green of the grass, the blue of the sky and the multicoloured pieces, the unmade jigsaw, of the people in between.

'Mum! Dad! Jamie!' He shouted their names as he ran, hoping against hope that if he didn't see them, they might hear him. He was half aware that people were looking at him, pointing at him, but he didn't care. He swerved round a man in a wheelchair. His foot came down in a bed of flowers. Somebody shouted at him. He ran on.

And just when he was about to give up, he saw them. For a moment he stood there, his breast heaving, the breath catching in his throat. Was it really them, just standing there? They looked as if they had been waiting for him all along.

But had he reached them in time?

Christopher was holding the camera. The lens cap was on. Jamie was looking bored. Elizabeth had been talking but seeing Matthew she broke off and gazed at him, astonished.

'Matthew...?' She glanced at Christopher. 'What

are you doing here? What's the matter…?'

Matthew ran forward. It was only now that he realised he was sweating, not just from the effort of running but from sheer terror. He stared at the camera in his father's hand, resisting the impulse to tear it away and smash it. He opened his mouth to speak but for a moment no words came. He forced himself to relax.

'The camera…' he rasped.

'What about it?' Christopher held it up, alarmed.

Matthew swallowed. He didn't want to ask the question. But he had to. He had to know. 'Did you take a picture of Mum?' he asked.

Christopher King shook his head. 'She wouldn't let me,' he said.

'I'm too much of a mess,' Elizabeth added.

'What about Jamie?'

'What about me?'

Matthew ignored him. 'Did you take a picture of him?'

'No.' Christopher smiled, perplexed. 'What is all this, Matthew? What's the matter?'

Matthew held up his hands. 'You haven't taken

a picture of Jamie? You haven't taken a picture of Mum?'

'No.'

Then – the horrible thought. 'Did you let them take a picture of you?'

'No.' Christopher laid a hand on Matthew's shoulder. 'We've only just got here,' he said. 'We haven't taken any pictures of each other. Why is it so important anyway? What are you doing here?'

Matthew felt his knees go weak. He wanted to sink on to the grass. He felt the breeze rippling past his cheeks and a great shout of laughter welled up inside him. He had arrived in time. Everything was going to be all right.

Then Jamie spoke. 'I took a picture,' he said.

Matthew froze.

'Dad let me!'

'Yes.' Christopher smiled. 'It's the only picture we've taken.'

'But...' Just four words. But once they were spoken his life would never be the same. 'What did you take?'

Jamie pointed. 'London.'

And there it was. The entire city of London. They were standing on a hill and it lay there, spread out before them. You could see it all from here. St Paul's Cathedral. The Post Office Tower. Nelson's Column. Big Ben. That's why the Kings had come here.

For the view.

'London...?' Matthew's throat was dry.

'I got a great picture.'

'London...!'

The sun had disappeared. Matthew stood watching as the clouds closed in and the darkness rolled towards the city.

light
MOVES

I suppose
my story begins
with the death
of a man
I never met.

His name was Ethan Sly and he was a journalist, the racing correspondent for the *Ipswich News* with his own column which was called Sly's Eye. He was, apparently, a thirty-a-day man – cigarettes, that is – and when he wasn't smoking he was eating, and when he wasn't eating he was drinking.

So nobody was very surprised when, at the ripe old age of forty-two, Ethan had a huge heart attack and dropped dead. In fact nobody even noticed for a couple of hours. He'd been working at his desk, typing up his tips for the Grand National, when that poor, overworked organ (his heart) had decided that enough was enough. The doctor said that it had probably happened too fast for him to feel any pain. Certainly, when they found him he just looked mildly surprised.

I learnt all this because my dad worked on the

same newspaper. I've always been a bit embarrassed by this. You see, he writes the cookery column. Why cookery? Why not football or crime or even the weather report? I know I'm probably sexist and Dad's told me a hundred times that most of the famous chefs are men but still...

Anyway, he was there when they cleared out Ethan's office and that's how I ended up with the computer. And that's when all the trouble began.

Dad came back home with it the day after the funeral. He was carrying it in a big cardboard box and for a crazy moment I thought it must be a puppy or a kitten or something like that. It was the way he was cradling it in his arms, almost lovingly. He set it down gently on the kitchen table.

'Here you are, Henry,' he said. 'This is for you.'

'What is it?' Claire asked. She's my little sister, nine years old, heavily into Barbie and boy bands. We don't get on.

'It's for Henry,' my dad repeated. 'You always said you wanted to be a writer. This is to help you get started.'

I had said – once – that I wanted to be a writer. I'd

just heard how much Jeffrey Archer earned. Since then the idea had stuck, and now whenever Dad introduced me to anyone, he said I was going to write. Parents are like that. They like labels.

I opened the box.

The computer was old and out of date. You could tell just from the way that the white plastic had gone grey. The keyboard was so grubby you could hardly read some of the letters and the plastic knob had fallen off the DELETE button, leaving a metal prong showing through. There were sticky brown rings all over the hard drive where the last owner must have stood his coffee mugs while he was working. It had a colour screen and a Pentium Processor but no 3D accelerator...which meant I could kiss goodbye to all the best games.

'What's that?' My mum had come into the kitchen and was looking at the computer in dismay. We live in a modern house on an estate just outside Ipswich and my mum likes to keep it clean. She has a part-time job in a shoe shop and a full-time job as a housewife and mother. She never sits still. She's always hoovering, dusting, polishing or washing. The cooking, of course, she leaves to Dad.

'It's a computer,' I said. 'Dad gave it to me.'

'Where did you get it?' She scowled. 'It needs a wipe-down.'

'What did you get *me*?' Claire whined.

'It's for Henry. To help him with his writing,' Dad said, ignoring her. 'They were clearing out poor old Ethan's office this morning and a whole lot of stuff was going begging. I got the computer.'

'Thanks, Dad,' I said although I wasn't entirely sure about it. 'Does it work?'

'Of course it works. Ethan was using it the morning he...' But then he shrugged and fell silent.

I carried the computer up to my room and made a space for it on my desk but I didn't turn it on then and I'll tell you why. I suppose it was kind of my dad to think of me and I know he meant well but I didn't like it. It was such an ugly old machine with its grey coiling wires and heavy sockets. Although I had tucked it away in the corner, it seemed to dominate the room. Do you know what I mean? I didn't want to look at it but at the same time I couldn't keep my eyes off it. And I had a nasty feeling that the empty, dark-green glass monitor...well, I almost felt that it was staring back.

I had tea. I did my homework. I talked on the telephone to Leo (my best friend). I kicked a football around the garden and finally I had a bath and went to bed. It sounds silly but the truth is I'd put off going back to my room as long as I could. I kept on thinking of Ethan Sly. Dead and rotting in his grave. And just forty-eight hours before, his nicotine-stained fingers had been pattering across the keyboard that now sat waiting on my desk. A dead man's toy. The thought made me shiver.

I fell asleep quickly. I'm normally a heavy sleeper, but I woke up that night. Suddenly my eyes were wide open and I could feel the cool of the pillow under my head. What had woken me up? There was no sound in the room except...now I could hear a low humming noise; soft and insistent and strange. Then I realised that there was a green glow in the room. It had never been there before. It was illuminating the movie posters on my walls – not enough to make the words readable but enough to show up the pictures. I turned my head, feeling the bones in my neck click as they rotated on my spine. My left cheek touched the pillow. I looked across the room.

The computer was on. That was what was making the humming sound. The screen was lit up with a single word in large capital letters stretching across the centre.

CASABLANCA

That made no sense to me at all. Casablanca. A city in North Africa. The title of an old film that always made my grandmother cry. Who had typed it on to the screen and why? I was more annoyed than puzzled. Obviously my dad had come into my room and turned the computer on while I was asleep. I suppose he wanted to check that it worked. But I was fussy about who came into my room. It was my private place and Mum and Dad usually respected that. I didn't mind him fixing the computer. But I'd have preferred it if he'd asked.

I was too tired to get out of bed and turn it off. Instead I closed my eyes and turned my head away again to go back to sleep. But I didn't sleep. It was as if someone had thrown a bucket of iced water over me.

This is what I had seen even though my eyes had refused to believe it. This is what I was seeing now.

The computer wasn't plugged in.

The plug was lying on the carpet with the flex curled around it, a good six inches away from the socket. But the computer was still on. I put two and two together and decided I had to be dreaming. What other possibility could there be? I shut my eyes and went back to sleep.

I forgot all about the computer the next morning. I'd overslept (as usual) and I was late for school for the second time that week. It was all just a mad scrabble to get into my clothes, into the bathroom before Claire, and into school before they locked the gates. After that it was the usual school routine: maths, French, history, science...with each lesson melting into the next in the early summer sun. But then something happened and suddenly school was forgotten and the computer was right back in my mind.

It was just before the last lesson and I was walking down the corridor and Mr Priestman (biology) and Mr Thompson (English) were walking the other way. Now everybody knew that Mr Priestman was a bit of a lad; down the pub at lunch-time, smoking in the toilet since they'd made the staff-room a no-smoking area, and off to the betting shop between lessons. Well he was grinning from ear to ear as he came out of his classroom and the other teacher must have asked him what he was so pleased about because this was the fragment of conversation that I heard.

'A hundred and fifty quid.' That was the Priest.

'What was that then? A horse?' Mr Thompson asked.

'Yeah. The two o'clock at Newbury. Casablanca came in at fifteen to one.'

Casablanca.

A horse.

Ethan Sly's computer.

I don't know how I managed to get through the last lesson – it would have to be religious studies, wouldn't it? – but as soon as school was over I found my friend Leo and poured the whole thing out to him. Leo is the same age as me, fourteen, and lives in the next street. He's dark and foreign looking – his mother came from Cyprus – and he's the cleverest boy in our class.

'All right,' he said when I'd finished. 'So the ghost of this racing journalist...'

'...Ethan Sly...'

'...came back last night and haunted your Apple.'

'It's not an Apple. It's a Zircon. Or Zincom. Or something...'

'He haunted your computer and told you the result of a race that was happening today?'

'Yes, Leo. Yes. What do you think?'

Leo thought for a moment. 'I think you've had a bit too much sun.'

Maybe Leo isn't as clever as people think.

That night I did my homework at double speed, wolfed down my supper and cut out my usual argument with Claire. I went up to my room as soon as I could, closed the door and plugged the computer in. There was a switch on the front. I pressed it, then sat back and waited.

The screen lit up and a line of text stretched itself across the glass.

Zincom System. Base memory 640K. 00072K extended.

It was just the usual computer jargon – nothing unusual about that. The screen flickered a couple of times and I found myself holding my breath but then the software finished booting itself and clicked into an ordinary word-processing programme; the electronic equivalent of a blank page. I typed my name on the screen.

HENRY MARSH

The letters sat there doing nothing. I typed a line of text, even though I felt uneasy doing it.

HELLO, MR SLY. ARE YOU THERE?

Again, nothing happened and I started wondering if I wasn't behaving like an idiot. Maybe Leo was right. Maybe I had dreamt the whole incident. On the screen, the little cursor was blinking, waiting for my next input. I reached out and turned it off.

But the computer didn't turn off.

I had cut the power. The whole thing should have shut down but even as I sat there staring, two words glowed on the screen in front of me. There really was something ghostly about the letters. They didn't seem to be projected on to the glass but hung behind it, suspended in the darkness.

MILLER'S BOY

That was the name of a horse if ever I'd heard one. I reached out for a sheet of paper and as I did so I noticed that my hand was shaking. I was actually terrified but I suppose I was too fascinated by what was happening to notice. And something else was already stirring in my mind. The computer had already predicted the winner of one race. Priestman had won one hundred and fifty pounds on Casablanca. And now here was a second horse. Maybe there would be others. Suppose I were to put money on them myself? There was no limit to the amount I could make.

I wrote the name down on the paper. At the same time the letters began to fade on the screen as if it knew they were no longer needed. A moment later they had gone.

I tracked down Leo in the first break at school the next day. He listened to what I had to say with his usual, serious face but then he shook his head.

'Henry…' he began in a voice that told me what was about to follow.

'I'm not mad and I'm not making this up,' I interrupted. 'Look…' I had bought the *Sun* newspaper on the way to school and now I opened it at the back where the races were listed. I stabbed at the page with a finger. 'There it is,' I said, triumphantly. 'The four-forty Bunbury Fillies Handicap at Chester. Number five. Miller's Boy.'

Leo peered at the newspaper. But he couldn't argue. There it was in black and white.

'The odds are nine to two,' he said.

'That's right. So if we put two pounds on it we'll get nine pounds back.'

'If it wins.'

'Of course it'll win. That's the whole point.'

'Henry, I don't think…'

'Why don't we go down to the betting shop after school? We can go there on the way home.' Leo looked doubtful. 'We don't have to go in,' I went on. 'But it can't hurt to find out.'

'No.' Leo shook his head. 'You can go if you want to but I'm not coming. I think it's a bad idea.'

But of course he came. Why else do you think he's my best friend?

We went as soon as school was over. The betting shop was in a shabby, unfriendly neighbourhood, the sort of place where there's always graffiti on the walls and litter in the streets. I'd only ever passed it on the bus and nothing would have normally made me want to stop there. It was part of a parade of three shops and the funny thing was that you couldn't see into any of them. On the left was an off-licence, its window covered by a steel mesh. On the right was a smoke-filled café with its window coated in grease. The betting shop didn't have a window. It just had a sheet of glass painted to look like a race-track. The door was open but there were plastic strips hanging down to stop people looking in.

There was a television on inside and fortunately it was turned up high enough for us to be able to hear the commentary. Leo and I hung about on the pavement trying to look innocent as the four-twenty Fulford Handicap came to its close.

'...and it's Lucky Liz from Maryland...Lucky Liz as they come to the finishing line...it's Lucky Liz...Lucky Liz...then Maryland then the favourite, Irish Cream...'

Now, even as I was hearing this a thought was forming in my mind. I shoved my hand into my pocket and found exactly what I knew was there. Two pounds. I'd washed the car, mown the lawn and cleared the table twice for that. Slave labour! But I was thinking of what Leo had said. If I put two pounds on Miller's Boy, I'd get nine pounds back when it won. I took the money out.

'Put it away!' Leo must have read my mind. 'You said we were only coming to look. Anyway, you're too young to bet. They wouldn't even let you in.'

And that was when Bill Garrett appeared.

Bill was famous at our school. For five years he had terrorised staff and pupils alike, never doing enough to get himself expelled but always walking close to the line. The fire that had destroyed the gymnasium had always been put down to him although nobody could ever prove anything, just like the theft of two hundred pounds from the Kosovo relief fund. It was said that when he left, aged sixteen, with no qualifications whatsoever, the teachers had thrown a party that had lasted the whole night. For a while after that, he had hung around the school gates, occasionally latching on to some of the younger kids for their dinner-money. But he had soon got bored with that and hadn't been seen for a while.

But here he was, strolling out of the café with a cigarette between his lips and an ugly look in his eyes.

He must have been eighteen by now but smoking had stunted his growth. His body was thin and twisted and he smelled. He had black curly hair which fell over one eye like seaweed clinging to a rock. Leo coughed loudly and began to edge away but it was too late to run.

'What are you two doing here?' Garrett asked, recognising our uniform.

'We're lost...' Leo began.

'No we're not,' I said. I looked Garrett straight in the eye, hoping he wouldn't thump me before I got to the end of the sentence. 'We want to put a bet on a horse,' I explained.

That amused him. He smiled, revealing a set of jagged teeth, stained with nicotine. 'What horse?' he asked.

'Miller's Boy. In the four-forty at Chester.' Leo was making huge eyes at me but I ignored him. 'I want to put on two pounds.' I held out the money for Garrett to see.

'Two pounds?' he sneered. Suddenly his hand lashed out, his palm slapping up beneath my outstretched fingers. The two coins flew into the air. His hand whipped round and grabbed them. I bit my lip, annoyed with myself. They were gone and I knew it.

Garrett jiggled the coins in his hand. 'Shame to waste it on a horse,' he said. 'You can buy me a pint of beer.'

'Let's get out of here,' Leo muttered. He was just glad we were still alive.

'Wait a minute.' I was determined to see this through. 'Miller's Boy in the four-forty,' I said. 'It's going to win. Put the money on the horse and I'll let you keep half of it. Four pounds fifty each…'

'Henry…!' Leo groaned.

But I'd caught Garrett's interest. 'How can you be so sure it'll win?'

'I have a friend…' I searched for the right words. 'He knows about horses. He told me.'

'Miller's Boy?'

'I promise you, Garrett.' Inspiration struck. I held up my watch, noticing that the time was 4:35. It was now or never. 'If it loses, I'll give you my watch,' I said.

Leo rolled his eyes.

Garrett considered. You could almost see his

thoughts reflected in his eyes as they churned around slowly in what passed for his brain. 'All right,' he said at last. 'You wait here. And if you move you'll be sorry.'

He loped into the betting shop, the plastic strips falling across behind him. As soon as he had gone, Leo turned to me.

'Let's run!' he gasped.

'He'd catch us.'

'We could catch a bus.'

'He knows where to find us. School…'

'I knew we shouldn't have come here.' The sadder Leo becomes, the funnier he looks. Right now I didn't know whether to laugh or cry. 'What happens if the horse doesn't win?'

'It'll win,' I muttered. 'It has to.'

The plastic strips parted and Garrett appeared holding a blue betting ticket. 'I just got it in time,' he announced. 'The race is about to start.'

'And they're off…!' The sound from the television echoed out on to the street as the three of us stood there, Leo and me not knowing quite where to look. I wanted to get closer to the door but at the same time I didn't want to seem too eager so I stayed where I was. I could hardly hear any of the commentary and the bits I did hear didn't sound too good. It seemed that a horse called Jenny Wren had taken an early lead. Borsalino was coming up behind. I didn't even hear Miller's Boy mentioned.

But then at the very end, when the commentator's voice was at its most frantic, the magic words finally reached me.

'And it's Miller's Boy coming up on the inside. Miller's Boy! He's overtaken Borsalino and now he's moving in on Jenny Wren. Miller's Boy...can he do it?'

A few seconds later it was all over. Miller's Boy had come in first by a head. Dave Garrett looked at me long and hard. 'Wait here,' he commanded. He went back into the shop.

Leo grimaced. 'Now we're in real trouble,' he said.

'What do you mean?' I retorted. 'The horse won.'

'That's exactly what I mean. You wait and see...'

Garrett came out of the betting shop. There was a smile on his lips but it wasn't a pleasant one. It's how you'd imagine a snake would smile at a rabbit. 'What's your name?' he asked.

'Henry Marsh.'

He held out a hand. There were three pound coins in the palm. 'Here you are, Henry,' he said. 'Three for you and six for me. That seems fair, doesn't it?'

It didn't seem fair at all but I wasn't going to argue.

'This friend of yours...' Garrett had lit another cigarette. He blew cold blue smoke into the air. 'You think I could meet him?'

'He's very shy,' I said.

'In the racing business, is he?'

'He used to be.' That was true, anyway.

Garrett placed a hand on my shoulder. His fingers dug into my collarbone, making me wince. 'It seems you and me, we need each other,' he said. His voice was friendly but his fingers were digging deep. 'You get the tips but you're too young to place the bets...'

'I don't think there will be any more tips,' I whimpered.

'Well if there are, you make sure you keep in touch.'

'I will, Garrett.'

His hand left my shoulder and clouted me across

the chin hard enough to make my eyes water. 'I'm Mr Garrett now,' he explained. 'I'm not at school any more.'

He turned and walked into the off-licence. I guessed he was going to spend the six pounds he had just won.

'Let's go,' Leo muttered.

I didn't need prompting. Together we ran to the bus stop just in time to catch a bus home. I don't think I'd ever been so glad to feel myself on the move.

That night the computer woke me up again. This time the screen carried three words.

TEA FOR TWO

I buried my head in the pillow, trying to blot it out, but the words still burned in my mind. I'm not sure how I felt just then. Part of me was depressed. Part of me was frightened. But I was excited too. What was happening was new and strange and fantastic. And it could still make me rich. I could be a millionaire a thousand times over. Just thinking of that was enough to keep me awake all night. It would be like winning the pools every day for the rest of my life.

I didn't tell Leo about the horse. He hardly spoke to me at school the next day and I got the feeling that he didn't want to know. I had thought about telling my mum and dad but had decided against it – at least for the time being. It was my computer but if I told them, they'd probably take it away and I wasn't ready for that. Not yet.

Bill Garrett was waiting for me when I came out of school. I was on my own – Leo had got a part in the school play and had stayed behind to rehearse. At first I ignored him, walking towards the bus stop like I always did. But I wasn't surprised when he fell into step beside me. And the truth is, I wasn't even sorry. Because, you see, Garrett had been right the day before. He'd told me I needed him. And I did.

He was friendly enough. 'I wondered if you'd had any more tips,' he said.

'I might have,' I replied, trying to keep the tremble out of my voice.

'Might have?' I thought he'd turn round and

punch me then. But he didn't.

'How much money have you got?' I asked him.

He dug into his pockets and pulled out a soiled five-pound note and a handful of change. 'About six quid,' he said. At a glance I could see there was nearer ten but as I told you, maths wasn't Garrett's strong point.

'I could turn that into…' I'd already checked the odds and now I made a mental calculation. 'One hundred and eighty-five pounds,' I said.

'What?'

'How much will you give me?'

'Out of a hundred and eighty-five?' He considered. 'I'll let you have thirty.'

'I want a hundred.'

'Wait a minute…' The ugly look was back on his face, although I'm not sure it had ever left it.

'That still leaves you with eighty-five,' I said. 'You put the stake down, I'll tell you the name of the horse.'

'What happens if it loses?'

'Then I'll save up and pay you back.'

We were some way from the school by now which

was just as well. It wouldn't have done me any good to be seen talking to Garrett. He sneered at me in his own special way. 'How do you know I'll pay you the money if it does win?' he asked.

'If you don't, I won't give you any more tips.' I'd got it all worked out. At least, that's what I thought. Which only goes to show how wrong you can be.

Garrett nodded slowly. 'All right,' he said. 'It's a deal. What's the name of the horse?'

'Tea for Two.' Even as I spoke the words I knew that there could be no going back now. I was in this up to my neck. 'It's running in the four-fifty at Carlisle,' I said. 'The odds are twenty-five to one. It's the outsider. You can put on ten quid of your own and another three from me.' I gave him the money I had won the day before.

'Tea for Two?' Garrett repeated the words.

'Come to school on Monday with the winnings and maybe I'll have another tip for you.'

Garrett gave me an affectionate clip on the ear. It was still stinging as he scuttled off down the pavement and leapt on to a bus.

Tea for Two romped home easily. I heard the result on the radio later that evening and went to bed with a grin that stretched from ear to ear. Seeing me so cheerful, my mum decided I must be in love and Claire spent a whole hour teasing me. Well, I'd show her when I was a multimillionaire! That night the computer stayed blank but I wasn't worried. Maybe Ethan still took the weekend off. He'd be back. For once I was actually looking forward to school and Monday morning. One hundred pounds. Put that on another horse at twenty-five to one and I'd be talking thousands.

But I didn't have to wait until Monday morning to see Garrett again. He came round the next day. He brought Leo with him. One look at the two of them and I knew I was in trouble.

Leo had a black eye and a bleeding nose. His clothes were torn and his whole face was a picture of misery. As for Garrett, he was swaggering and stalking around like a real king of the castle. I'd forgotten just how bad his reputation was. Well, I was learning the truth now and at the worst possible time. Dad was at the newspaper. Mum was taking Claire to her dancing lesson. I was in the house alone.

'Where is it?' Garrett demanded, pushing Leo through the open front door.

'What?' I asked him. But I knew.

Garrett was in the house now. I wondered if I could make a dash for the upstairs phone and call the police before he broke several of my bones. It seemed unlikely. He slammed the door.

'I'm sorry…' Leo began.

'It had to be something special,' Garrett explained. 'I knew, you see. Nobody can predict winners. Not twice in a row. Not for certain. So there had to be some sort of trick.' He lit a cigarette. My mum would kill me when she smelled the smoke. If Garrett hadn't done it first. 'I knew you'd never tell me,' he went on. 'So I popped round and visited your friend. Took him out for a little chat. Well, he didn't want to tell me neither so I had to rough him up a little bit. Made him cry, didn't I.'

'There was nothing I could do,' Leo whispered.

'This is my fault,' I said. Right then I would have given Garrett the computer just to get him out of the house.

'So then nancy-boy starts telling me this story about a ghost and a computer,' Garrett went on, puffing smoke. 'You know...I hit him some more when he told me that. I didn't believe him. But he insisted and you know what? I began to think it must be true because when I threatened to pull his teeth out he still insisted.' Garrett turned on me. 'Is it true?'

'Yes.' There seemed no point in lying.

'Where is it?'

'Upstairs. In my room. But if you go up there I'll call the police.'

'The police?' He laughed. 'You invited me in.'

He took two steps towards the stairs and I hurried over, blocking his way. Now a streak of crimson crept into his face and his eyes took on the dead look of a police Identikit picture. 'I know your parents are out,' he hissed. 'I saw them go. You get out of my way or I'll put you in hospital. You wait and see what I'll do.'

'He means it,' Leo rasped.

'It's my computer!' I cried.

Garrett threw a handful of crumpled bank-notes at me. 'No. You sold it to me for a hundred pounds.

Remember?' He grinned. 'It's my computer now. You're too young to gamble anyway. It's against the law. You ought to be ashamed...'

He pushed past me. There was nothing I could do. Leo looked on miserably and I felt a bitter taste in my mouth. This was all my fault. How could I have been so stupid?

'Leo...' I began. But there was nothing I could say. I just hoped that we would still be friends when this was all over.

'You'd better go up,' Leo said.

I hurried upstairs. Garrett had already found my room and was sitting at my desk in front of the computer. He had turned it on and was waiting as the system booted itself. I stood in the doorway, watching.

'All right,' Garrett muttered. He balled his fist and struck down at the keyboard. A tangle of letters appeared on the screen. 'Come on, come on, Mr Ghost!' He slapped the side of the monitor. 'What have you got for me? Don't keep me waiting!' He hit the keyboard again. More letters appeared.

DBNOYEawES...

'Come on! Come on!' Garrett clasped the monitor in two dirty hands and pressed his face against the glass. 'You want to end up on the scrap-heap? Give me a name.'

I was certain nothing would happen. I had never asked for a horse's name to come up. It had just happened. And I had never been as greedy as this although I realised with a sick feeling in my stomach that given time I might well have become as hungry and horrible as Garrett was now. I was sure nothing would happen. But I was wrong.

The tangle of letters faded away. Two words took their place.

LIGHT MOVES

Garrett stared at the screen as if it was only now that he really believed what Leo had told him. The cigarette fell out of his lips and he giggled. His whole body was shaking. 'Light Moves.' He rolled the words on his tongue. 'Light Moves. Light Moves.' He seemed to notice me for the first time. 'Does this thing give you the odds?' he asked.

'No,' I said. I was defeated. I just wanted him to go. 'I get them in the paper.'

'I'll get them at the betting shop.' Garrett stood up. His hand curled round the flex and he yanked the plug out of the wall. The screen went blank. Then he scooped up the entire computer, holding it against his chest. 'I'll see you,' he said. 'Enjoy the hundred pounds.'

I followed him back down the stairs. Perhaps I could have stopped him but the truth is that I didn't want to. I just wanted him to go.

Leo opened the front door.

'Goodbye, suckers,' Garrett shouted.

He ran out and over the road. There was a squeal of tyres and a terrible crash. Leo and I stared at each other, then ran outside. And even now I can still see what I saw then. It's like a photograph printed into my mind.

Garrett had been hit by a large white van which had come to a halt a few yards from our front door.

The driver was already out of the cabin, looking down in horror. Garrett was lying in a pool of blood that was already widening around his head. His arms and legs were splayed out so that he looked as if he were trying to swim across the tarmac of the road. But he wasn't moving. Not even to breathe.

The computer which he had been carrying when he was hit was smashed beyond repair. All the king's horses and all the king's men wouldn't put Zincom together again. Glass from the monitor was all over the road. The casing around the hard disc had split open and there were valves and wires everywhere; electronic spaghetti.

All of that was horrible, but do you know what was worse? It was the name on the side of the removals van. I saw it then and I see it just as clearly now.

G.W. FAIRWEATHER REMOVALS LTD

And beneath that, in large red letters:

LIGHT MOVES.

More Orchard Black Apples

❏ The Phone Goes Dead	*Anthony Horowitz*	978 1 84616 972 4	£3.99
❏ Killer Camera	*Anthony Horowitz*	978 1 84616 971 7	£3.99
❏ Burnt	*Anthony Horowitz*	978 1 84616 966 3	£3.99
❏ Scared	*Anthony Horowitz*	978 1 84616 968 7	£3.99
❏ The Night Bus	*Anthony Horowitz*	978 1 84616 967 0	£3.99
❏ Twist Cottage	*Anthony Horowitz*	978 1 84616 973 1	£3.99
❏ Little Soldier	*Bernard Ashley*	978 1 86039 879 7	£4.99
❏ Revenge House	*Bernard Ashley*	978 1 84121 814 4	£4.99
❏ The Snog Log	*Michael Coleman*	978 1 84121 161 9	£4.99
❏ The Drop	*Anthony Masters*	978 1 84362 196 6	£4.99